Prince William

Dedicated with appreciation and admiration to
Joyce Murphy, DVM
and the hundreds of other volunteers who worked so hard to save
the lives of animals and birds caught in the huge Alaskan oil spill.

Prince William

Gloria Rand
Illustrated by *Ted Rand*

Henry Holt and Company ✦ New York

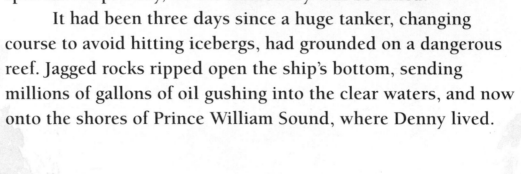

W here's Dad? Isn't he having breakfast?" Denny asked.

"He left early," her mother replied. "He took our boat out to help set containment booms around the fish hatchery. If that spill isn't kept away, all the salmon fry will be killed."

It had been three days since a huge tanker, changing course to avoid hitting icebergs, had grounded on a dangerous reef. Jagged rocks ripped open the ship's bottom, sending millions of gallons of oil gushing into the clear waters, and now onto the shores of Prince William Sound, where Denny lived.

"Remember, when you go out today, stay away from the beach," Denny's mother warned. "I don't want you near that oil. Do you understand?"

"Okay, Ma," Denny answered.

Denny understood, but who would notice if she just looked? Her father was gone, and her mother would soon be back on the telephone, lining up volunteers to help clean shore birds found covered with oil. Denny grabbed her heaviest sweater and headed out the door. What would the beach be like? She had to see.

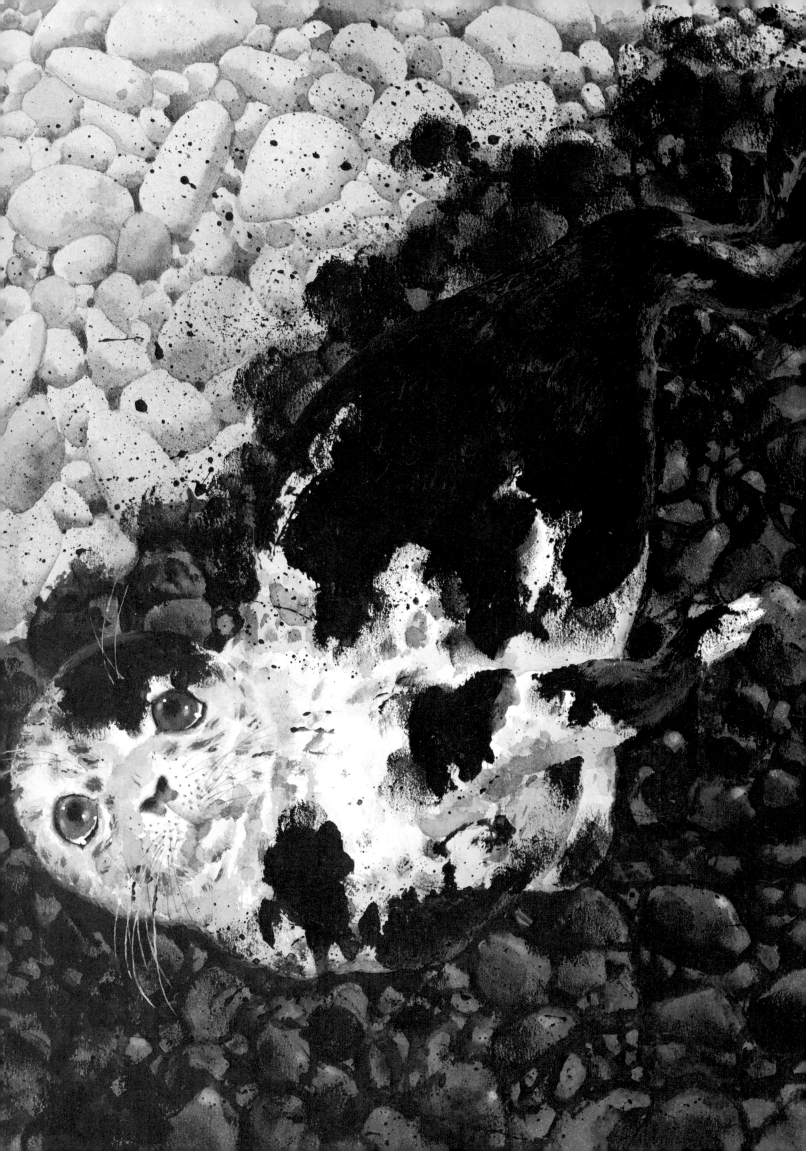

From a low bank above the shore, she saw rocks covered with thick goop, and pools of black stood in puddles on the sand. The air had a bad oily smell. Denny held her nose.

Suddenly from far down the beach, Denny heard a faint cry, the cry of a little baby. She heard it again.

Denny scrambled out to the water's edge, slipping over slimy rocks, and stumbling through sticky sand. There she found what was making the pitiful sounds. It was a seal, a baby seal.

"Oh, you poor, poor puppy." Denny pleaded as she tried to comfort the tiny creature, "Don't cry, please don't cry."

The oil-coated baby seal was hard to hold, and almost impossible to pick up, but Denny did both. Then she gently bundled it into her sweater, and carefully picked her way back across the slippery beach toward home.

"I'd better warn you," she told the pup. "My mother is going to be very cross with me. But I couldn't have left you out there on the beach, could I?"

When Denny stepped onto the cabin's back porch, her mother scolded her. "I told you to stay away from the beach. Weren't you listening at all? And look at you, you're tracking oil all over the place!"

"Ma, don't be mad," Denny cried. "Look what I found." Denny unfolded her sweater. "It's a baby seal."

Denny's mother carefully took the pup in her hands.

"This baby is barely alive, but still breathing. We'll do our best to save its life."

Together they launched a skiff and headed across the bay. Denny's mother knew that a rescue center had been set up in the town's school gym. She was certain that someone there could save this seal.

The gym was a busy place. As fast as they could, volunteers were cleaning and caring for hundreds of oil-covered birds and otters.

"What have we here?" an animal doctor asked as she carefully lifted the baby seal out of Denny's sweater. "Looks like a sick little boy to me, a little boy about ten hours old."

"It's Prince William, I just named him," Denny announced. "He's not going to die, is he?"

"Not if we can help it," the doctor replied. "But you've certainly had a rough start in life, haven't you, Prince William?"

The tiny seal answered with a weak whimper.

Denny watched as the doctor and another volunteer went to work. They gave Prince William sugar water to make him stronger, washed his coat with gentle soap, and then rinsed him over and over again in salt water.

"I'm taking Prince William to our animal hospital," the doctor explained. "He's very ill, and needs to be put in an incubator for a few days, just like a human baby. It's a warm, safe place where he'll find the air easier to breathe. While he lives there we'll give him lots of fluids, vitamins, and special medicines."

"Will I ever see him again?" Denny asked.

"Of course," the doctor said. "Come visit in a few days. He'll be feeling much better by then . . . won't you, little fellow?"

That night a fierce storm began to blow. By morning the oiled waters had churned themselves into miles and miles of brown froth.

"Look, Ma," Denny gasped as she stared out the window. "Come look! Our beach is covered with chocolate pudding."

"That's what it looks like," her mother sighed. "But it's just whipped-up oil, dirty, filthy oil."

A few days later, Denny and her mother went back to town. They saw a lot happening along the way.

"See those people dressed in bright suits? They're washing oil off the beaches with pressure hoses," Denny's mother explained. "The oil goes back into the water. Then it's sucked up by big skimmers and hauled off to a disposal site, where it can't do any more harm."

Later she showed Denny other workers who were cleaning beaches by hand. They were wiping oil off each rock and log with heavy rags. Farther on, dead and dying birds and other creatures littered the shore.

Denny wished they could watch the workers longer, but her mother had promised to wash birds at the rescue center. Then they were going to visit Prince William!

In town, the sidewalks were crowded with people who had come to help clean up the spill. Cars and trucks jammed the streets, and all kinds of boats were packed into the harbor. Planes, one after another, were flying into the airfield nearby.

At the rescue center Denny watched gulls, murres, kittiwakes, and otters being washed.

A sick deer was brought in, but it died a few minutes later.

"That deer must have eaten kelp tainted with oil," someone said quietly. "I didn't think she would pull through. I've seen it happen before—bears and their cubs, wolverines and eagles. You name it, they're all being poisoned by the spill."

Death, dying, and sickness seemed to be everywhere. Denny felt sadder and sadder.

"Can't we go now?" she finally begged her mother. "I really want to see Prince William."

At the animal hospital, Denny raced down the main hall toward the incubator room. Prince William's incubator was empty!

"Oh no, Prince William is dead too!" she cried.

"Don't worry," Denny's mother said calmly. "We'll find the doctor. She'll know where he is; and if he's okay or not."

They hurried to the doctor's office.

"Your pup is doing just fine," the doctor assured Denny. "Why don't you come and see for yourself? We're teaching him to eat herring and to swim, just like his mother would do if she were here. Would you like to watch his swimming lesson?"

Denny followed the doctor into a large room where a volunteer was moving the little seal back and forth in a big tub of water. Every now and then she held him under running water.

"Why is she doing that?" Denny asked.

"So someday when he's back out in the wilderness he won't be afraid of waterfalls," the doctor smiled. "He's going to learn how to swim in a bigger pool too, so he won't be afraid of deeper water either."

"Prince William won't ever be afraid of *anything*," Denny replied proudly.

As the weeks passed Denny visited Prince William
often. When he wasn't swimming they took walks down the
hospital halls together. As he grew bigger, Prince William cried
less and barked more, his own special way of talking.

One day Denny brought Prince William his own stuffed
toy, a fuzzy little seal. Prince William chewed and sucked on the
toy, just like any baby.

"Prince William will soon be ten weeks old," the doctor told Denny one day. "It's time for him to go back to the sea, and to his relatives. Would you and your mother like to come along?"

It wasn't easy to put Prince William back where he belonged. First he had to be flown to Halibut Cove. Then he had to get used to the waters there, waters much colder than he liked. At first he cried a lot, and kept climbing out onto a nearby dock. But in a short time Prince William was ready to swim free.

Near a rocky point, the little seal was put into
sparkling clean water. At first he stayed close by, but
as he became used to his new surroundings he swam
farther and farther away.

"I'm sure going to miss him." Denny tried to
smile. "It's really hard to say good-bye, isn't it?"

"It's always hard to say good-bye to a good
friend," her mother said softly. "I'm sure Prince
William is going to miss you too. You're the best
friend he'll ever have, that's for sure. You saved
his life, Denny."

At that moment Prince William popped up beside the boat Denny and her mother had rowed out in to keep him company.

"See, I'm doing just fine," he seemed to say. Then he swam off to join his wilderness family.

Author's Note

There is a real Prince William. There are also Princesses Diana, Fergie, Victoria, and Prince Philip, all healthy survivors of the Alaskan oil spill.

Their recoveries, and those of other seals, were made with the help of local schoolchildren. These young volunteers raised money by collecting recyclable paper and cans, selling popcorn, and by getting pledges from their parents. All the money accumulated went toward the purchase of herring, a food rich enough to supply the fast-growing pups with the right diet. Towels and blankets, for the seals' care and comfort, were also collected.

Following major clean-up efforts, and the earth's own natural ability to heal itself, waters of Prince William Sound once again sparkle and the beaches appear to be clean. But globs of oil still lie under seashore rocks, and the spill's long-term effect on the wildlife will not be known for many years to come.

Text copyright © 1992 by Gloria Rand. Illustrations copyright © 1992 by Ted Rand.

Published by Henry Holt and Company, Inc., 115 West 18th Street, New York, New York 10011.
Published simultaneously in Canada by Fitzhenry & Whiteside Ltd.,
195 Allstate Parkway, Markham, Ontario L3R 4T8.
Library of Congress Cataloging-in-Publication Data
Rand, Gloria. Prince William / by Gloria Rand; illustrated by Ted Rand.
Summary: On Prince William Sound in Alaska, Denny rescues a baby
seal hurt by an oil spill and watches it recover at a nearby animal hospital.
[1. Seals (Animals)—Fiction.   2. Wildlife rescue—Fiction.   3. Oil spills—Fiction.   4. Pollution—Fiction.
5. Alaska—Fiction.]   I. Rand, Ted, ill.   II. Title.
PZ7.R1553Pr   1992   [E]—dc20   91-25180

ISBN 0-8050-1841-7 (hardcover)
1   3   5   7   9   10   8   6   4   2
ISBN 0-8050-3384-X (paperback)
1   3   5   7   9   10   8   6   4   2

First published in hardcover in 1992 by Henry Holt and Company, Inc.
First Owlet paperback edition, 1994

Printed in the United States of America on acid-free paper. ∞